Chasing

BUTTERFLIES

A Standalone Novella

Bad Girls: Book One

By Jennifer Labelle

Chasing BUTTERFLIES

Limitless Publishing, LLC
Kailua, HI 96734
www.limitlesspublishing.com

Formatting: Limitless Publishing

ISBN-13: 978-1-64034-468-6

Dedication

To all my supporters,

You make this writing experience worthwhile and I hope you enjoy my little twist on this story as much as I have.
And remember, always chase those butterflies to the happily ever after you deserve.

Prologue

Sawyer

"Whatever the reason you dragged me here, consider it your Christmas gift." Sawyer Maddox grimaced as she fingered the lacey undergarment in front of her. Love was in the air and although she was extremely happy for her sister, it made Sawyer sick to be around Carley. It brought back way too many memories from a time she wished she could forget.

Sewer, sewer, sewer...

Sawyer cringed from the memory and quickly moved on. They'd already been to lunch, a shit ton of clothing stores because her sister needed to find the perfect outfit for her date tonight, and now they were stuck in an overpriced underwear shop. She couldn't wait to leave.

Ah, the things you do for family.

She sighed.

"Don't think I won't take you up on that *bi-atch.*" Carley laughed and gave her a big hug.

1

"Did I say Christmas? I also meant birthday, too." She smirked.

"Nice one, smart ass." Her sister stuck out her tongue and laughed. "If you're offering, then get out that credit card and follow me." Carley grabbed a heaping pile of lace, satin, and see-through thingies and Sawyer groaned as her sister dragged her to the fitting rooms lounge. It felt like torture while her sister tried on clothes and she impatiently waited in a chair just outside, twiddling her thumbs. Unlike some people, she hated to shop.

"So, seriously though, what's the occasion for this sudden emergency girly crap—shopping spree we've got going on here?"

"You've been hanging out with Toby way too much lately," her sister mumbled. "Sometimes I feel conflicted on whether that's a good thing or a bad thing."

Toby James was Carley's long-time beau, Sawyer's mentor, and the best guy she'd ever met so far, and that was saying a lot. He'd make a great brother someday and she was genuinely happy her sister had found someone worthy for a change. It also didn't hurt that he was a kick-ass tattoo artist and had taught Sawyer almost everything she knew about the art of skin canvassing.

"Whatever." Sawyer rolled her eyes.

"He's got something special planned later and I have a feeling he might propose." She squealed in excitement. "I'm not absolutely sure or anything. It's just a hunch. So keep your fingers crossed."

"Wow, Carl. That's big, honey." Sawyer sat up and smiled. Her sister's excitement was contagious

2

and it made the whole day bearable suddenly. Sawyer hated shopping. "I've got everything crossed for you, if it means you'll be happy."

Carley opened the fitting room door holding up two scraps of sheer material. "Found it!" She held them up for inspection and closed the distance to embrace her again. "Thanks, Saw-saw. You're like the daughter I never planned for but totally glad I got stuck with." She sniffled and Sawyer laughed. It was a long-standing joke they shared when things became too mushy. Sadly, it was also the truth and Sawyer loved her for it more than words could express.

Carley Maddox was five years her senior, thirty to her now twenty-five years old and had been raising Sawyer since she could ever remember. Carley was the one who held the family together when their parents were too drunk or high to move, let alone take her to school or make sure they had food on the table. She was her rock; the only family she had that meant anything and the only one she'd do anything for and then some.

"Ditto punk." Sawyer winked and her smile fell away when Carley's expression turned serious.

"Promise me you won't always shut out love. I want you to have what I do someday. Toby brings out the best in me. To this day, even three years later, I swear I can still feel the butterflies in my stomach whenever I even think about him, let alone when I'm close to the man. And don't roll your eyes at me." She crossed her arms in admonishment and Sawyer fought her instinct to laugh by biting her bottom lip. "I know you're young and having fun but mark my words, the one-night stands will get old and I don't want to see you end up all alone. Do you hear me?"

"Yes, Mom. I hear you." Sawyer saluted. "I'm fine, Carl. Now stop depressing yourself with my shit and hold onto those butterflies you just talked about." She grabbed the flimsy lingerie from her sister's hand and headed straight for the register, knowing Carley would follow close behind.

Thinking back on that day, she remembered how she couldn't wait for it to be over, so she could escape again in her art and tattoo designs. Although genuinely happy for Carley's happiness, Sawyer was also envious and it pissed her off.

Love, pffft...

Never again. It just wasn't in the cards for Sawyer. Of that, she was pretty sure. If only she knew it would be the last good memory of being with her sister she'd ever have.

Things hadn't turned out as Toby and Carley had planned that night. He'd proposed, all right, but instead of the blissful night it should have been, it turned out to be a clusterfuck of chaos, despair, and heartbreaking anguish for all.

Carley died that night in an accidental fire caused by several candles that had been lit for ambiance. Toby was wracked with guilt for surviving when she hadn't and Sawyer needed to run. So, run she did, to the one place she never thought she'd set roots in again...home.

Goodbye Minnesota. Hello again, Hill Country, Texas.

Chapter One

Sawyer

It was her first day back, and already, Sawyer wondered if she'd made a big mistake. After losing Carley, she felt like she'd been suffocating. Toby was a wreck and she couldn't stand to watch him fall apart when she was doing the same inside. Not only had he lost Carley, but he had also lost his tattoo shop that horrible night, and now the only family that had ever mattered to her was gone too.

It was time for a brand-new start.

Deciding to go back to Kerrville had been an instinct. Sawyer needed to travel home eventually to sell the old homestead anyway, and as a bonus, she'd also get to show everyone she'd made it despite the odds. It's just too damn bad she was stuck with all the bitter-sweet memories.

Here goes nothing.

Her childhood house was boarded up and abandoned since her parents' passing the year before.

The small, overgrown lot of land needed a good trim and the structure needed a lot of fixing up before she'd be able to get rid of it. It was mostly cosmetic, though. Sawyer let herself inside and coughed as she dropped her bags by the door. Thank God she had remembered to stop by the store to pick up supplies on her way over. Dust particles danced in the air and she was already exhausted just thinking about how much time it would take to make the place presentable. She stepped further inside, wiped her finger across the railing on the stairs, and wanted to gag when about an inch of dirt encrusted itself onto it. There were cobwebs in almost every corner and raggedy sheets draped over the little furniture that remained inside.

Sawyer sighed, it had been a long trip home and there was so much to do. There was no way she'd be able to sleep in this hell hole the way it was, so she took on the task of cleaning up. She blared music from her phone and sang along to the lyrics on her playlist. It wasn't so bad. The kitchen was the first place on her list to disinfect and after about an hour or two in that room, it was decent enough for her to move on to something else. She figured her bedroom would be next, so she headed upstairs. Memories good and bad flooded through her as she walked past Carley's old room and Sawyer broke down. The paint was chipping off the purple painted walls, the wood floors creaked as she stepped inside, and there was an old stinky mattress on the floor just where she remembered it.

They didn't have much growing up, but they at least had each other. Tears streamed down her face and she wiped her nose with her hand before taking a deep breath. "And now I'm alone." She whispered her thoughts out loud and made the decision that it was break time. She needed to escape her own pity party and there was a stiff drink out there with her name on it, so she got the hell out of Dodge to claim it.

It didn't take her very long to reach her destination.

A country song played on the jukebox while she sat at the old-fashioned wood bar in the front of Tipsy's. It was packed, which is why she'd chosen the place to begin with—to hide inside the crowd. With a beer in one hand and her phone in the other, she'd been preoccupied with looking up commercial properties in the area to set up her shop. It would preferably have an apartment she could occupy, as well, so that when she fixed her folks' old place up, she could sell it.

The place was rocking with an even mixture of hot cowboys and bikers. It was a unique crowd, but she totally fit in, which was rare. Sawyer sighed as she spotted the cutest couple near the mechanical bull on the other end of the bar. They sort of reminded Sawyer of how Toby and Carley had been together.

"Another drink?" A beautiful redheaded woman asked from behind the bar.

Sawyer startled and nearly choked mid-swig. She coughed and wiped her mouth. "Uh, sure…" she said and put her phone away. She could use another one.

"The name's Tonya." The bartender smiled as she gave her another beer. "You new around here?"

"Yes and no." Sawyer intentionally kept her

answer vague. "Grew up close by. Left as soon as I could. Now I'm back." The truth was, even when she lived here way back when, she'd purposely avoided most people. She was still, to this day, a bit of a misfit but that was all part of her charm.

"Sounds like there's a story there," Tonya said. Sawyer laughed humorlessly.

"You have no idea. I'm Saw…"

"This must be my lucky night." Sawyer had goosebumps the minute she was interrupted. The deep baritone coming from the stranger next to her was sexy as hell and he had a body to match. *Whew!* His face was partially hidden underneath the baseball cap he sported. Man, he was built nicely: tall, thick, and muscular. His dark t-shirt fit snugly, accentuating his pecs, flat stomach, and tanned arms. She could bet he also had a tight little ass in those Wranglers too. It was hard to tell now, seeing as he was sitting on it but…

"And why is that Jagger Hale? Hm." Tonya asked.

Sawyer straightened and her face flushed. *Oh, hell no. Of all people, why him?*

"I'm in the company of two gorgeous women. Why else?" Jagger responded. "I'll have whatever's on tap when you have a chance, Sugar."

"Coming right up."

As Tonya left to get him his drink, he turned his seat in her direction. "I'm still amazed by that woman." He said, tilting his head towards the pretty bartender, completely oblivious to her uncomfortable posture.

"Why is that?" Sawyer asked before chugging half of her drink.

8

Please don't recognize me, please don't recognize me.

"She's near deaf but doesn't let it stop her. It's remarkable." He said shaking his head. He looked away and back to Sawyer again. "Hey, you all right?" He went to touch her arm and withdrew quickly as she cringed away.

"Couldn't be better," she lied. Jagger chuckled. It was as if he hoped to lighten the mood. He flicked his hat up so she could see his eyes and he gave her the once-over with his gaze.

"Hm," he grunted as he rubbed the stubble on his chin. "Do I know you from somewhere? You look familiar and it's not like me to forget a beautiful face."

"I get that all of the time. I guess I just have one of those faces." She lied again and shrugged while trying her best to play it cool.

"If you say so, darlin'." He smiled and turned towards the bar again as Tonya set the frosted mug of golden brew in front of him. Sawyer watched him take a sip and sigh from the corner of her eyes.

"Besides, if you can't figure it out, I'm not going to willingly give up the information." She grumbled. It must have been liquid courage that made her speak up like that. "I think I should just go. Later, stranger."

She was halfway to the exit when he called out, "Hey, wait up," and reached for her arm to catch up. "I'll walk you out."

"It's not necessary. Besides, you just got your drink." She pointed towards the bar and dropped her hand.

"You're better company," he replied. "Humor me,

will you?"

"Fine, but you're not going any further than the parking lot."

"It gives me an extra minute to figure you out." Jagger shrugged. Sawyer cursed under her breath as he led the way. Not only was his ass better than she remembered, but she could also still feel the pull between them even after the many years apart.

Jagger Hale was trouble with a capital T, at least, where she was concerned.

The music from inside was a distant hum now. It was dark out with a million pretty stars up above. She could feel Jagger's curiosity about her deep down inside and she was at a loss for how to proceed. They had history. Although short, it still lingered in her mind. It was a quiet two seconds before Jagger broke the silence with, "Nice ink you've got there." He gestured towards the half sleeve she had on her right arm and she couldn't help but smile.

"Thanks. I love my art on the body and off it." She closed her eyes and took a deep breath before she opened them again. It had been a long day. "Do you have any?"

"Tattoos?" He lifted his eyebrow and smirked. "One, but I'd have to take off some clothing for anyone to see it."

Damn it! He's flirting.

"Jagger," Sawyer said as if she was exasperated with him already, but secretly she was wondering where the tattoo was located on that delicious body of his. Not that she'd ever admit that out loud, or anything.

"That's my name. Speaking of, I never did get

10

yours," he said just as they reached her car.

"Uh, huh. Now if I gave you that, the mystery would be over." Her keys jangled as she grabbed them from her pocket, but Jagger leaned against the driver side door before she could open it. "And, right now, I'm still unsure if you'd like what I had to say. Best to play it safe, I think." She took a step forward, hoping he'd take the hint and move out of her way, but the stubborn stud wasn't budging.

"I don't know any man who doesn't like a challenge, sweetheart, and I will figure you out. So, consider me intrigued." He smiled and stood straighter. "Now, how much have you had to drink?"

"What?" She asked totally taken off-guard by the question. "I am not drunk." Hell, it had taken her over an hour to finish her first beer and she hadn't even finished her second one.

"Let me be the judge of that." He held his hand out and wiggled his fingers. "I have a feeling we've met before. I just can't seem to place it yet and if that's the case, you know I'm a decent guy. So, I think maybe you should pass me your keys and I'll make it my duty to get you home safely."

"Absolutely not!" She said, gripping them tighter.

"You need references, darlin'? If so, feel free to march back inside and get as many as you need. I know almost everyone inside, including the owner," he said.

Sawyer was in complete shock. So much so that her mouth was literally hanging open.

Of all the nerve...wow.

She fidgeted and narrowed her eyes at him. "There's no need. I appreciate your concern but I'm perfectly capable of taking myself home."

He chuckled in response and crossed his arms. The smooth tan skin and bulging muscles of his forearms distracted her and she muttered another curse under her breath. Sawyer looked back up at his face and he winked.

Busted!

"Humor me," he repeated. "Are you always this pigheaded? Or is all of it reserved just for me tonight?" He held out his hand again. "Come on. Just consider this some good old southern hospitality. You get home safely and I feel better about it."

"Fine. It's not like I've been given any other choice." She handed him her keys and stomped her feet as she made her way to the passenger side. "Stubborn? Huh!" She huffed. "Takes one to know one."

"It's all just part of the package," he teased. Once they were inside and all buckled up, he turned towards her. "Now, where to?"

Sawyer gulped as she looked into those hypnotizing green eyes of his. At that moment, she knew she was royally screwed. Because as soon as she gave him the address to her folks' place, he'd know exactly who she was and that might not be a good thing at all.

Chapter Two

Jagger

Well, hell.

It took a minute before recognition hit, but when she'd given him the address to the Maddox house, Jagger knew. It had to be her.

Sawyer freakin' Maddox.

When he had walked into the bar earlier, he'd noticed her right away. Now he knew why. She was the one.

The one who got away.

"You're shitting me, right?" Jagger couldn't think of anything else to say. He'd thought about her over the years; thought about what he'd say if he ever saw her again, and he always wondered if there'd ever be an opportunity to right his wrongs.

"Now, why would I do that?" She growled and crossed her arms over her very ample breasts.

Damn, what a nice rack. Come on Jag, get your head out of your ass and quit screwing this up.

He didn't answer at first and instead started the ignition to get going before she bolted. She seemed even more skittish than she had been earlier, but now he knew why, so he just shrugged and thought of what to say next.

Uh...damn it!

"Sewer?" She stiffened and he winced.

Way to go, dumbass.

He didn't mean to call her that it just slipped out. Okay, maybe he was just looking for a reaction to make one hundred percent sure he had the right woman.

He did all right.

"It's Sawyer." Her voice broke as she said her name and she fidgeted. Her hands were fisted at her sides. She was upset, rightfully so, considering he'd just brought up history, bad history, by calling her that name. He had caused that and it made him more desperate to fix it. "Stop the car."

"I'm really sorry, honey. I don't even know why that slipped out."

"Do you need me to refresh your memory? Because mine is quite clear. Stop the car, Jagger!" Her voice rose as she spoke and she took a deep breath. Her fists were so tightly closed, her knuckles were white. She looked like she was ready to hit something or someone.

"We're almost there. Can we at least talk about it? I know I don't deserve it, but could you just give me a chance?" Jagger asked. Damn, she was beautiful, even in anger.

Sawyer began to laugh. It was sort of hysterical, yet bitter. "You're joking, right? Because if not, you're out of your damn mind. As far as I'm concerned, you can shove it."

He nodded once and his jaw tensed in frustration. She was so damn hard-headed and he needed a minute to come up with a plan. He had to believe she'd hear him out eventually.

"Fair enough." He took a deep breath. "For now."

"Good, now drop me off, leave me alone, and go bug Tonya for all I care." Sawyer loosened her grip and folded her arms across her chest again. She was looking out the window now and missed the look of surprise that came across his face.

Where the heck had that come from?

"Bug Tonya?" He repeated it like it was a question and she turned around to face him again.

"Yeah, she's amazing, remember? So, ask her out, or whatever it is you do, and stay the hell away from me."

Was she jealous?

The thought made him smirk because maybe there was hope after all between him and the little fireball in the next seat. Her driveway was coming up, so he had to make this fast. "First of all, Tonya is a married woman. And second, she's only ever been a friend. Now you, on the other hand…"

"Don't!" Sawyer held up her hand and he sighed.

"I'm sorry, Sawyer. I've been waiting a long time to tell you that." He pulled up to her driveway and the moment the car stopped moving, she grabbed the keys from the ignition and was out of there.

Jagger climbed out and quickly caught up before she could slam the front door in his face. "I thought about you over the years. Always wondered what

15

happened to you, where you went. Wondered what I'd say if I got a second chance."

Sawyer stopped just shy of the front porch but didn't turn around. "Why are you telling me this?"

"Because I screwed up when I let you go." He ran his fingers through his hair and prayed for God to give him strength. "I'm not the guy you thought I was."

"I know, and that's what was, and still is, the problem." She turned around and he could see she was about to cry but was holding it back. "I…I can't do this, Jag. So just do us both a favor and go. Forget you ever saw me."

She didn't give him a chance to respond. Sawyer was fast when she wanted to be, that was for sure. As soon as those words left that beautiful mouth of hers, she was gone.

Dang it!

Jagger sat on the front porch steps and called himself a cab as he thought about the day a long time ago that started all the misery between the two of them.

Eight years ago, they'd been dating for two months and he was determined to make it a night to remember. He'd planned it for weeks, in fact. Jagger didn't have wheels yet, so a buddy of his had lent him the keys to his truck and he was taking Sawyer camping for the night. He hoped to show her how special she was to him because he was falling hard.

It was all set up. He was taking her to his favorite spot. It was a small clearing on the large spread of land his family owned by the Guadalupe River. He'd gone earlier to set up a small tent. He'd bought flowers, packed a cooler full of goodies in the back seat for them, and a box of condoms, just in case. The last one was probably wishful thinking on his part but he was keeping his fingers crossed and wanted to be prepared for anything.

Her long dark hair flew around her face from the wind through her open window as he drove. She was mesmerizing. He kept taking peeks at her from across the cab as she tilted her nose up in the air and closed her eyes and took a deep breath. God, she was beautiful. Her golden eyes sparkled as she smiled widely at him and licked her lips. "Try keeping those eyes on the road, cowboy." Sawyer laughed. "So where is it you're taking me, anyway?"

"You'll see soon enough," he teased. "We're almost there."

"Fair enough." Sawyer sighed and looked out the window at the landscape passing by. "Thank you, by the way. I'm pretty sure I've never said so, and I want you to know how much I appreciate what you do for me. It's peaceful when we're together, refreshing from my kind of normal, considering who my parents are."

He was taken off-guard by her statement at first, but then understood where it was coming from. The two Maddox girls were legendary, it seemed, but not in the way you'd think. There were always rumors floating around about them. Rumors about their lifestyle and their family mostly, but Jagger never paid any attention to the gossip. Rumors were just that, not fact and just because you came from bad stock didn't mean that you were bad.

Her sister Carley was older and from what he

could tell, took the brunt of the family problems onto herself. She took care of Sawyer and had gotten into trouble with the law a few times while doing it too. Money was tight, he assumed, their house was falling apart, and Sawyer kept to herself until recently. He showed an interest and the quiet girl with the pretty dark hair, slim figure, and hand-me-down clothes wasn't so inconspicuous anymore. It had taken him a bit to get through to her though, but eventually, he had worn her down and she had finally agreed to go out with him. They had been a couple ever since.

"Then I need to thank you for the same because you're amazing, Sawyer, and I'm lucky as hell to have you with me." He winked and she blushed.

Dirt from the road flew up from the tires, making a small cloud of debris on each side of them and the river flowed up ahead. One right turn and they'd be there, nothing but nature, water, and appreciation for his girl. It was going to be awesome.

He pulled up to the clearing and watched her take it all in as he parked the truck not far from where he'd set up the tent. Her entire face lit up and before he knew what hit him, she leaped into his arms from across the seat. "It's beautiful, Jag. I can't believe you did all of this for me."

He chuckled and she squeezed him tighter. This girl deserved everything but he knew she wasn't used to being cared for by anyone other than her sister. Jagger sobered his expression and lifted her chin when she leaned back so she'd look into his eyes. "I did this because I wanted to give you an escape, although brief. I also brought you here because I love this spot and I wanted to share it with my favorite girl." He opened the door, slipped out of his seat, and gathered her into his arms. She squealed with delight as he carried her to the blanket he had laid there just before he'd left to pick her up and put her down in front of it. He set her on her feet and then started walking backward. "Stay there. I'll be right back."

He jogged to the truck again, leaned in, and grabbed the cooler of food and drinks along with the bouquet of yellow roses and jogged back to her again. "I figured you might be hungry, so I thought we could eat first then maybe take a swim later." Her eyes locked onto the roses, so he handed them to her. "These are for you."

"Wow," she whispered as she brought them up to her nose to smell. "They're beautiful."

He nodded and before he could respond, the cooler dropped so he could catch her. Her legs wrapped around his waist, the flowers were suddenly behind his head, her right hand was in his hair, and her lips plastered against his in appreciation. Sawyer hadn't wasted any time probing the slit of his mouth with her tongue and the kiss turned heated in an instant. She squirmed against him and the chubby he sported ached to be set free from the confines of his pants.

They were both breathless when they pulled apart. Jagger held on to her tighter as he dropped to his knees and gently sat her down beside him. "As much as I love kissing you, sweetheart, I think we should slow down a bit before we hit the point of no return." He adjusted himself and Sawyer turned a nice shade of pink again. "I don't want there to be any regrets later on if we get carried away." The zipper imprint against the head of his cock and the blue balls he'd surely have to battle be damned.

As if on cue, her stomach growled and it made them both laugh. "Okay, we'll put the kissing on hold, so you can at least feed me," she teased and he smiled wider. "So, what have you got?"

"That's my girl." He smirked. "We've got pulled pork sandwiches, salsa and chips, some of mom's chili for later, and pecan pie." Jagger handed her a bottle of water and let her help herself to the food. They ate in comfortable silence and twenty minutes later, he was packing the cooler back into the truck again, so they didn't attract any unwanted wildlife.

"So, you mentioned swimming." Sawyer wrapped her arms around him from behind and squeezed.

"I sure did." He loosened her grip, so he could turn around to face her and was blinded for a second by the hot afternoon sun that shone brightly behind her. It sort of looked like she had a halo, his angel. Jagger caressed the side of her face. "You ready to go take a dip, baby?"

Sawyer nodded. "It's hotter than blue blazes out here." She stepped back and smiled as she took off her shirt. "Funny thing, but it seems I don't have a suit."

Jagger was stunned while rooted to the spot. He couldn't take his eyes off her and he groaned when the shorts came off too. Well, hell. That was totally unexpected, yet a very welcome sight to behold. Just as he'd gotten his dick tamed through lunch, it now saluted them both proudly once again.

Sawyer stood in nothing but her simple bra and underwear for only a second longer before she ran ahead yelling, "Last one in is a rotten egg!"

"Oh, you asked for it." He laughed and nearly fell over as he quickly tried to rid himself of his Wranglers. Her head start beat him to it, but he wasn't far behind when jumping in. The cool water was refreshing and he dove under so he could come up on her other side. She squealed again, splashed him, and laughed so hard his heart felt like it expanded just by watching her. She was happy and it was a good look on her. He splashed back and then swam closer. Jagger wrapped her in his arms and rubbed his nose against hers right there in the middle of the river. "You look happy as a hog in mud right now."

"All thanks to you," she whispered and tilted her head to give him a quick kiss. One peck turned into two before she nibbled on his bottom lip. "I need you, Jag."

"I'm right here, darlin'."

"I'm grateful." She tilted her head. "But what I meant to tell you was that I'm ready. So, let's get carried away past the point of no return. Love me with that sexy body."

She didn't have to tell him twice. They quickly swam to shore and he carried her caveman-style once they were on dry land again. Sawyer now hung over his shoulder upside down. He couldn't wait to get her naked. She giggled the whole way to the tent and he squeezed her ass once he let her upright.

Sawyer moaned.

"You sure about this?" he asked. He'd been dreaming about this moment for so damn long but for her, he'd wait as long as it took for their first time together. No regrets.

"Very," Sawyer answered and it was all the confirmation he needed. They crawled inside and he zipped up the flap to keep the bugs out. His girl was already ready for him to close the distance between them but he took a moment to admire her lying on his sleeping bag. Her brown hair spread against his pillow and the wet bra and panties set she wore left nothing to the imagination. Her rosy nipples puckered for him and he couldn't take the wait any longer, so he joined her.

Jagger slowly crawled on top of her and captured her lips hungrily. She was his addiction, his drug, and as young as he was, he knew he'd never tire of her taste. Their tongues caressed, mouths pressed together, and the skin on skin contact was their undoing. He sucked on her bottom lip before trailing his own across her jaw. He slowly moved lower and lower with his mouth, down her neck, and didn't stop until he came face to chest with her delectable tits. On instinct, he pushed the cups of her bra aside and licked around her hardened nipple. Sawyer arched her back to get closer and encouraged the action by holding on to the back of his head.

"Oh, God Jag. Please don't stop."

He loved how responsive she was to his touch. Her hips moved across his thigh, humping him and he could feel the warm dampness from between her legs. Fuck, his dick ached. "I won't baby, but I need to get you ready, so it won't hurt as much."

"Please…" She thrashed her head to the side and writhed while he paid attention to the other boob. Sawyer gasped and the noise made him smile against her. He continued his pursuit lower, kissing his way down her stomach to her panty line. He slid the undergarment off and tossed them into the corner.

"Take off your bra." He grunted and then spread her legs wider to admire her fully. She was so moist her pussy glistened. "You are so beautiful."

Her breathing turned rapid while his fingers explored her body. He slid through her slippery pink folds and inserted his index finger inside. There was a wet spot now on his boxer briefs from his own pre-cum and his fingers were slick with Sawyer's juices. It was time to stop fucking around and make her come. He inserted another finger to stretch her and furiously pumped them in and out. She was so fucking tight. Jagger shifted so that he was beside her now. He wanted both access to her breasts and pretty little cunt at the same time. His thumb circled her clit, Sawyer's breath hitched, and she was moaning like crazy for him. He felt like he was ten feet tall. She deserved to feel good and he wanted to make her feel that way, but it was the moment his lips touched her again that she exploded. He kissed his way across her chest, paying extra close attention to her breasts until the orgasm drifted and she was a boneless heap.

"That was amazing," she moaned. "Just give me a minute and it'll be your turn, okay?

"I'm cocked and loaded, sweetheart. Play too much and I'll be sure to explode before we get started." He reached over to grab the box of condoms he'd gotten earlier. "You can explore me all you want the next time I swear it, but right now I just need to be inside you."

She nodded and he rushed to get fully naked and

sheathed with protection. Jagger crawled on top of her, the head of his cock nudged her opening and his teeth clenched when his dick slowly slipped inside. He stopped when he reached her virginal barrier and looked into her eyes. God, but it was bittersweet torture to hold himself back. "You still okay?"

"More than ever," Sawyer whispered. "I want all of you."

He surged forward in one smooth stroke to the hilt, it was uncomfortable for a minute and then it was pure bliss.

Later that night, they sat by the fire pit and ate chili from the thermos he'd brought. Sawyer was dressed in his shirt that looked way better on her than it did him and a pair of shorts you could barely see from beneath the hem. Sexy. Jagger sat on the log beside her half-dressed and never happier.

"Jag, you out here buddy!"

Sawyer stiffened and he cursed. A few buddies from football and their girlfriends came through the trees to the clearing with beers in tow.

"There you are," Dylan said and laughed when his gaze clashed with Sawyer's.

Jagger held her hand and squeezed. "What the hell are you doing here?"

"Give you my truck and that's the thanks I get?" His friend feigned a wounded look and staggered back while the girls around him giggled.

"Figured I wouldn't be interrupting much." Dylan leered. "Have you met Stacy?" He dragged a cute little blond from behind him and Jag wasn't having any of it.

"Look." He narrowed his eyes. "I appreciate the

help with the truck but if you don't mind I'd like to spend some time with my girl alone."

The others seemed to ignore the hint when one put on some music from her phone. Two other guys began tossing cans of beer around, Dylan laughed, and his perfect night turned to shit.

"Saw your mom in town today, Sawyer," Stacy said, disgusted. "Lookin for her next fix, I guess. Her hair was matted. She had the twitches and it looked like she hadn't showered in a month. Don't any of y'all wash?"

Sawyer looked mortified and it made Jagger growl but he was proud when she stood up for herself. "Every day. We're nothing like her," she said, talking about her mom. Sawyer was one of the strongest people he knew and Jagger was proud of her.

Stacy wasn't finished. "I doubt it. Why the heck are you with this girl, anyway, Jag? She's trash just like crack heads she calls parents. Might as well start calling her 'sewer' and Carley can be 'maggot.'"

Suddenly, their unwanted company began chanting the word "sewer" and began laughing. He went after Dylan angrily for bringing them all here and in his moment of distraction, he hadn't noticed that Sawyer went into the tent, grabbed the truck keys, and sped out of there like a bat out of hell.

He was fucked.

On the way home, a very distraught Sawyer had gotten arrested for grand theft auto. Dylan reported his truck stolen, knowing Sawyer was driving. She spent a night in jail and Jagger had whipped Dylan's ass until he agreed to drop the charges. Shortly after she was released, she'd up and disappeared on him without a word.

***

The cab finally showed up to take him to his truck parked at Tipsy's and he jumped in, sat back, and began thinking they weren't seventeen anymore. Eight long years had come and gone and now that his mind was back to the present day, he threaded his fingers through his hair in frustration. He knew Sawyer thought he'd used her back then, had maybe put his friends up to it that night so long ago, but she was dead wrong and he was determined to prove it to her. The night they shared had been special. She'd given him a gift and he was determined to get that second chance.

But, first he needed a plan.

Chapter Three

Sawyer

"It's about damn time," Toby growled through the phone line and Sawyer's heart ached. Dang, she missed him something fierce. He was like family, her big brother, or at least he would have been if he'd gotten the chance to marry Carley. Sawyer fought the longing and forced back the emotion coming forth just from hearing his voice again. A few weeks had gone by since she'd left and this had been the first opportunity to call him. She could say it was because she'd been so busy with the house and finding a commercial property for the new business, among other things, like distracting thoughts of Jagger. *Damn him.* Truthfully though, she'd been avoiding Toby to escape her feelings of despair. He made her think of Carley and she hated getting emotional.

"Miss me that much already, have you?" She teased, her voice cracked, and she hoped that he couldn't hear the inner turmoil in her voice. He had enough of his own shit to get through.

"You know it. How you doing out there, baby girl?"

"I'm surviving." Sawyer cleared her throat. "Good news is, I finally found the place for Mad Ink." She decided to honor her sister's memory by naming the tattoo parlor after them. Mad was just an abbreviation of their last name. It was time to take a stand and show this town what she was made of. She wasn't the same Sawyer Maddox from all those years ago. She was a fighter. "It's small but it's right in the tourist district of downtown Kerrville. Good foot traffic."

"That's awesome. Mace is getting antsy again and looking for a change. I should send him your way for the extra help," Toby said, talking of a mutual friend who worked for Toby at Blank Canvas. "The renovations just started up here, so it'll be a while before we get back at it, anyway."

"Hell yeah. Tell him to call me and we'll figure it out. It'll be nice to see a familiar face. Speaking of renovations, how'd it go with the production company?" Thanks to the infamous Ash Harris, lead singer of the rock band Love the Sinner, and Toby's cousin, Blank Canvas had become a part of reality TV. Shortly after Ash showed off his new ink during an interview with MTV, they were known worldwide. The problem now was there wasn't a shop to film in anymore. It had burned down the night Carley died and Toby had to rebuild.

Toby sighed. "Better than expected, actually. They let me off the hook. Contract was up for renewal, anyway, and I'm done with that shit show for now."

"I hear you. The reconstruction will be busy enough both personally and in business," she agreed. "I'm swamped, too, getting my own empire fixed up."

"I hope you practice what you preach, sweetheart, because we both know we're fucked up." Toby laughed bitterly. "Enough about this personal garbage. Tell me more about you and Mad Ink."

"With pleasure, my brother from another mother." She couldn't agree more. They'd both deal with their grief in their own time and until then, there was so much to do. "I've got equipment ordered, the landlady is painting, the place has got a modern flare, and I'm stoked to get started already. Mace will be a bonus. I'll send you pictures as soon as I can. On another note, the landlady is amazing. Her name is Becca, and she seems cool. They have this annual arts and crafts event that she's hosting and she asked me if I'd be interested in contributing. I figured I could kill two birds with one stone here by showing off my insane art skills and promoting the business all at once. I'm planning on doing freehand portraits, but I'll also have my portfolios on the table and business cards handy to give out."

"It sounds like you've got it all put together," he said. Sawyer could swear he was smiling when he told her this. "I'm proud of you, kid, and I know your sister would have been too."

"Thanks, Tob. It means a lot coming from you."

There was a knock on the door and she thanked God for small miracles because this conversation was getting too real. At the mere mention of her sister, she became choked up and would prefer to have her meltdown in private. "There's someone at the door. Can you just hang on for a sec?"

"Sure," he replied.

Sawyer set the phone down on a small table near the entrance of her childhood home and opened the door to discover yet another delivery guy. "Can I help you?"

"Package for Sawyer Maddox. Sign here, please." The man handed her a clipboard and gave her a long white box after she passed it back. She took the parcel inside and grabbed the phone again.

She'd seen Jagger on her very first night in town and he'd been respectful enough of her wishes to keep his distance, but it still hadn't stopped him from sending her gifts every day since. She suspected this was another one.

"Hey, Toby. Sorry about that." She answered the phone again and cradled it on her shoulder. She sat on the couch and read the card as she listened to him reply.

Still thinking of you and hoping for that second chance to explain.

XO

Jag.

"Anyone important?"

Yes. "No," she replied. "It's sort of complicated. Do you remember that guy I told you about? The one I foolishly fell in love with when I was younger."

"Yeah," Toby growled. "Do I need to go down

there and kick somebody's ass?"

"I don't think so." She chuckled. "Anyway, I ran into him on my first night here and he's been sending me gifts ever since. Wants a chance to explain some things to me, blah, blah, blah…"

"That who it was?" he asked.

"Delivery guy." Sawyer bit her lip while she proceeded to open up the latest gift.

"What's he been sending?"

"A fresh delivery from a bakery in town of pecan pie. One day I'd been at the shop to check out progress before the opening and had lunch delivered for me–pulled pork. Little things like that." She pulled the ribbon loose and peeked inside the box. "Looks like the gift of the day is a dozen yellow roses."

"Sounds like he's hooked." Toby snickered. "Try not to break his heart too badly."

"Yeah," she whispered. Her heartrate picked up speed and she just about melted on the spot. All these gestures were memories from when they were a couple, some of her favorites, and she hadn't pieced it together until she saw the bouquet. Her butterflies were beginning to act up, as Carley had once put it, and she didn't know if she could go down that road again. It would crush her worse this time if it went bad, which is why she'd stuck to the one-night hookups ever since. Word spread fast around small towns, so it wasn't hard for him to figure out how to find her when he wanted to. The question was, did she want to be found? "He's trouble with a capital T, but nothing I can't handle."

"No doubt." Toby laughed. "Listen, I gotta go for

now. I'm heading over to see Mamma Deuce and I'm meeting up with Carson. Be on the lookout for Mace's call, will ya? And keep in touch, squirt."

"Whatever." She rolled her eyes. "Love ya, Tob. Send Mamma D my love too."

"Yeah, me too."

Sawyer hung up the phone and sat up to smell the roses. She thought of Jagger all the time since running into him again. Not that she'd admit that out loud and these sweet gestures were beginning to wear her down. Maybe she'd agree to hear him out to get closure, but she needed to be on guard because he was dangerous for her heart. He'd been the only man she ever loved and if she wasn't careful she could totally see herself coming undone.

***

Jagger

It was as hot as Hades in here. Jagger turned off the welding torch, flipped his mask up, and tore off his gloves before checking out his work. He was filthy, sweating something fierce, and probably smelled to high heaven, yet he had never felt better. There was always a high after finishing a project, especially one as good as this. A specially designed horse trailer he planned to drop off to a client tomorrow afternoon. One more job down and it was on to the next. It was a gift. An art created with his own hands. And he loved every moment of it.

Jagger smiled with satisfaction and decided to clean himself up just a bit, maybe get something to eat before he painted the ranch's insignia on the side of it as a personal touch for his client. He left his work space and walked home, loving how close it was. He'd bought a couple of acres of land on the family ranch and started Hale's Customs right out of one of the old barns. He'd built a five-bedroom, three-bathroom, luxury home right beside it that looked more like a large log cabin. The entire structure was mostly made of wood and stone. It had taken months to fix it up to his liking, but it all worked out in the end way better than he could have hoped. He was proud of it.

Once inside, he tore off his drenched shirt. He sighed and headed straight for the kitchen. He washed his hands and grabbed a cloth to clean off some of the sweat and grime on his body too. There was no sense in taking a shower until his work was done, he thought. He tossed aside the rag, grabbed the fixings to make himself a sandwich, and took a cold bottle of water from the fridge. It only took a minute or two to make lunch and as he stood in front of the island in the middle of the room he took a big bite. Now that he wasn't busy, he thought of Sawyer again. The woman had been a major source of his thoughts for the past eight years, probably even longer, and now that she was back…well, he couldn't let her go. Not again. Not until she at least heard him out. He wondered if she'd gotten the roses he'd sent yet.

Jagger smiled, thinking of her reaction and prayed she'd give him a shot. Come hell or high water, the woman would hear what he had to say…eventually, because he hadn't thought of a plan B if this idea of his didn't pan out.

***

Sawyer

Sawyer googled him and pigs were surely about to fly. Mr. Jagger Hale of Hale's Customs had done good for himself and it made her happy to know it. If someone had mentioned a month ago that she'd be intentionally looking him up, she'd have told them they were out of their damn minds. But there she was, driving down a country road to see the man.

Was she crazy? Probably.

Curious? Most definitely. And she had acted on an impulse.

Once she'd finished her phone call with Toby, she'd felt too melancholy and needed an escape. The Jagger she once knew was incredible at distractions and she desperately needed a break from the pain of losing the only family she had left.

She was all alone in the world.

After putting all but one of the roses in a vase, she'd gotten the information she'd needed from her phone and entered it into her GPS, hoping she wouldn't be interrupting anything too important.

About ten minutes later, she stood in front of a beautifully refurbished barn listening to loud country music coming from the inside. Sawyer leaned against the door and admired the shirtless, sexy cowboy busy at work. His dark hair was tousled as if he'd run his fingers through it several times. His tanned skin glistened, oily and slick, and a few drops of sweat ran from his temples down to his pecks going lower across his washboard abs. Sawyer licked her lips. Taking advantage of the opportunity to ogle him without being caught, her gaze continued south. Thick thighs, a fine ass, and a very nice bulge was encased in blue jeans that molded him to perfection.

Sweet Lord!

She fanned herself and gripped the rose in her hand tighter as she walked inside to make her presence known. "Knock, knock." It hadn't taken long for him to notice her. His eyes widened and he pulled the white mask down that was covering his mouth and nose, tossed it aside, and he smiled. Her heart swelled and she took a deep breath to calm her nerves.

Jagger turned off the music.

"Got your gift." Sawyer held up the single flower she'd brought and sniffed it. "They're beautiful. Thank you."

"Had to get your attention somehow." He shrugged. "Still have to talk."

"I know." She sighed. "And I suppose we will. What ya working on over here?" She'd decided to give him a chance once she realized how persistent he'd become to gain her attention, but she needed to take it slow before they got into anything heavy. The past was hard for her to relive. She was better than that now. She was no longer the trash they all thought she was.

"Just finishing up with the trailer," he said.

"It looks amazing, Jag. Double Deuce?"

Jagger nodded. He'd gotten the brand from the sign as you entered the Wyatt ranch. His work was his own form of art and he liked to add a few personal touches for each individual customer. It was large uppercase letters of double D meshed together with a small letter W at the bottom. He'd been able to spruce it up by giving it a 3D effect.

"Wow, so you're like, a jack of all trades, huh?" Sawyer smiled and nudged his arm with her shoulder. From what little she'd read about his business, she knew he was a welder, but when she'd arrived, she'd seen him painting this on the side. It was impressive.

"Sort of." He grinned back. "Enough about me. I'm more interested in you right now."

"Really?" She stepped closer, so close she could smell him, and nearly groaned. There was that magnetic pull again that she remembered. Fate was such a fickle little bitch.

"It's good to see you." He nodded and reached out to tuck a lock of hair behind her ear.

"You know, I'm on the phone with Toby catching up and talking about Carley, and then there's someone at my door with a note and these gorgeous flowers. It got me thinking about the other sweet gestures from you and you succeeded in gaining my attention again. It was perfect timing too." She took a step away from him, so she could pace while she continued. "Lord knows I love Carley with all of my heart, but there's so much going on, I can't think about her right now. It hurts too much. Do you know what it's like to lose everything important to you?"

"Who's Toby?" Jagger asked. It made her laugh so hard.

"Out of everything I just said, your main concern

is who Toby is?" She giggled. "You're priceless, Jag. I can't remember a time when I've laughed this hard. It's been so long."

She needed a minute.

"I'm confused. One, I most definitely would like to know who this Toby is? It may be none of my business but there you have it. Second, what the heck happened between you and your sister to make you hurt like that? And three, I do know what it's like to feel like you've lost the best thing in your life. It's how I felt when I lost you." Jagger stepped closer and reached for her hand. "I never knew about Dylan's plans to ruin our night, and I'm sorry for everything that happened afterward too. I kicked his ass when I found out you'd been arrested until he agreed to drop the charges, but when I went to find you, you were already gone. I loved you, Sawyer, and then you just up and disappeared on me without a word."

Wow!

Sawyer held her breath and let it all out in one loud exhale. "Toby was engaged to Carley. He's like a brother to me and taught me everything I know about tattooing. And, my sister..." She choked up and looked away, so she could compose herself. She shook her head to clear her thoughts. "If what you say is true, then I'm sorry, Jag. I guess I just thought you were too good to be true. I had low self-esteem and not the best upbringing. My own parents didn't even care and when the people who were supposed to be your friends started calling me names and talked about my parents, I felt like the trash they all deemed me to be. Figured you used me that night. So, when the charges were mysteriously dropped, we ran to start over because it hurt too much to stay."

He tugged her close again to give her a hug and when she looked up at him, he looked anguished, so she acted on instinct and kissed him with everything she had. Enough talking for now. It was time for that escape, Sawyer style.

Their chemistry was off the charts. She wanted to climb on him and lick him from head to toe like a big ol' lollipop. There was no going slow. It'd been way too long. The second their lips touched, it was like an inferno ignited between them. She was burning up. The kiss was hungry, a mixture of tongue and teeth, fast-paced, and she was craving him to be as close as possible. Her fingers tangled into his hair and she whimpered when he pulled away.

"Sawyer?" His chest rose and fell rapidly as they both tried hard to catch their breath. "You sure about this?"

"What I need is to stop thinking so hard, Jag, and right now, this feels right." She stood up on her tippy toes and went back in for another taste of his mouth.

"Just..." She kissed him again between his words until he gripped her hands and began walking her backward towards his desk. Her butt hit the edge of it and she jumped to sit on top, spread her thighs, and wrapped her legs around his middle to bring him flush against her moist center. Her nipples puckered and she was breathing hard with want when he continued to talk. "Hold on a sec. I really like where we're headed, sugar, but if you'd like to continue, I think we need to take this to a shower." He grimaced and he moved his hand between them up and down so she could focus on his sweaty body.

Sawyer grinned and instead of a reply, she showed him what she'd fantasized about doing from the moment she walked into the bar when she hopped off the desk and licked him from his belly button to his earlobe. "Mm, you taste good just the way you are, right here, right now."

Jagger shuddered as if he had a chill and groaned. He picked her up so she could wrap her legs around him again and he thrust his hard cock against the spot she needed him most. Sawyer matched his rhythm and dry-humped him right back. With one arm, he cleared the top of his desk and laid her on top of it.

"Damn!" he said, sounding frustrated. "I need to grab a condom. They're in the house."

"Taken care of already." Sawyer shook her head and took the protection out of her front pocket. "A girl can never be too prepared." More like, old habits die hard. She was always prepared when it came to sex. She'd certainly had it often enough. A girl had her needs too and she was always careful.

"I like a woman who thinks ahead." He smirked. "Now, where were we?"

"Pretty sure we were about to get naked." She licked her lips and whipped her shirt off while he helped her get her shorts and underwear off. Afterward, she admired the view while he tore off his jeans, taking his boxer briefs off along with them. He quickly sheathed himself with the latex rubber and teased her with the tip of his dick against her clit. "Fuck, yes. Don't stop." Her nipples puckered. She moved her bra cups aside and played with her breasts.

"You are so damn sexy. Always have been but

now…" He grunted. "Shit, Sawyer, I want to savor you so bad but I'm not sure I can go too slow."

"I'm with you, Jag. Fuck me, baby. We'll do sweet some other time." She writhed underneath him and gasped as he rubbed her nub harder. She was close.

"Come for me first. You want my cock? Show me how much and I'll give it to you." His teeth clenched, his muscles strained, and he licked his lips like he wanted to devour her. "Now, sugar. Now," he demanded.

She obliged his request by exploding in bliss.

He thrust balls deep inside her pussy while she pulsed against his shaft and he held still until it subsided. He moaned her name and made her feel special because, despite his earlier confession, he started off slowly to give her time to get used to his girth and length until she encouraged him to fuck her faster.

He was incredible.

Sawyer knew she was in trouble.

She thrust her hips in tune with his again to keep up and cried out when his mouth got reacquainted with her breast. "Oh, God, Jagger, you feel so good."

His pace picked up and he thrust deeper, pushing out all of the way and slamming back in again. The desk rocked. She was in Heaven and he shuddered through his own release, filling the condom inside of her a moment later. It was just the fast, hard fuck she'd needed. Their slick bodies molded together as Jagger collapsed on top of her to catch his breath.

Sawyer was rocked to her very core. There was always something special between her and Jagger.

Their union tonight solidified it and that scared the crap out of her. To think that she left to start over because of a misunderstanding hurt, but at the same time, it made her the strong woman she was today, so maybe it was for the best. It was all too confusing. One thing was for sure, she could totally fall in love with this man again. Heck, he'd only been back in her life for a very short time and her feelings were strong, so maybe she hadn't stopped loving him at all. Maybe she just chose to ignore it because she was devastated to lose him, to begin with. To her embarrassment, she became so overwhelmed with emotion, she started to cry.

He must have felt her tears fall on him. "Hey," he whispered with concern, "I didn't hurt you, did I?"

"No," She croaked as she covered her face with her hands. "Please let me up."

He scrambled to get off her and helped her to stand. "What's the matter?"

She needed a minute while she got dressed to compose herself, so he gave it to her. She watched him put on his own clothes and appreciated his patience. "It was a little too good." She said and laughed at her own silliness. "I'm sorry, Jag. I'm just a little messed up right now and no good for you. Thank you for tonight because I needed to be loved, if only for a short time, but I gotta go."

"Sawyer, wait. Please don't go." He reached for her, but it was too late because she ran…yet again.

Damn it!

Chapter Four

Jagger

"Corbin and Carter Dean! Stop fighting and step away from your daddy's stand before you break something!" Lena warned just as Jagger approached his sister's table. He couldn't help but chuckle. They were at the art fair and those little hellions had their momma wrapped around their little fingers and they both knew it. Lena was such a sweet soul, but his nephews were also a handful when they wanted to be.

Her face softened the instant the boys apologized and did as they were told.

"We're bored." Corbin pouted and his brother-in-law Alex laughed alongside Jagger and shook his head.

"I am one lucky man," Alex exclaimed.

Jagger felt a pang of envy for a second but brushed it off.

"That you are," he replied. "Hey, Lena. Do you

remember Sawyer Maddox at the table over there?" Jagger inclined his head toward the woman of his dreams across the lot. "I hear she's doing portraits, if you want to take the boys over."

Her face lit up, she grabbed the twin's hands, and walked their way. "You don't say?" She smirked. "She any good?"

"You betchya," Jagger answered. He hadn't seen Sawyer's work yet but he had no doubt she'd be amazing at anything she chose to do. It didn't hurt that he'd noticed she had a steady flow of occupants over there either.

She nodded, "Good enough for me. I'm gonna just take the boys for a walk, go say hi, and try and tire them out." She winked at him and a second later, Alex had her in his arms to kiss before she went anywhere. They were so crazy in love and one day Jagger hoped he'd be so lucky with his own woman someday.

"Hey, man. Thanks for dropping the trailer off yesterday. It looks great." Darrel Wyatt walked up to them and clapped Jagger on the shoulder while he watched his sister approach Sawyer's table.

"No problem." Jagger looked at the man quickly and shrugged. He'd become instantly distracted by the beautiful brunette Lena was currently talking to. Hell, Sawyer had been the source of his thoughts day and night especially since she seemed to be back for good this time. That was, if her opening a tattoo shop meant anything. It had been two days since their romp in his workspace; forty-eight long ass hours of waiting for her to come around.

Alex noticed his pre-occupation and smiled

widely. "She looks a little familiar but I'm not sure from where."

"Yeah," Jagger grunted. "Used to be local, then she left." He sighed and lifted his hat to drag his fingers through his hair before he put it back on. "She kept to herself mostly back then though and tried to stay invisible to everyone except me."

"Hm," Darrel said, rubbing his chin. "Name?"

"Sawyer Maddox."

Darrel nodded. "That explains it. Knew Carley a little, a long time ago. Messed up hand they were dealt with their folks." He shook his head. "Heard about what happened in the news last month too. It's a damn shame."

Jagger's curiosity was peaked. "What happened last month?" He hadn't heard anything from the news about Sawyer, so he wasn't sure what Darrel was talking about. It was the first time he'd taken his eyes off Sawyer since he'd arrived at the Kerrville art fair.

"Big fire out in Minnesota. It was the tattoo place from that popular show, what's it called?" Darrel thought for a minute and snapped his fingers when it came to him. "Blank Canvas with Toby James! Anyway, the place was a total write off." He shook his head, looking somber. "Carley died in that fire, Jag. You didn't hear?"

Fuck!

"Naw." He gulped. That explained so much. His heart broke for her. Jagger cleared his throat to dislodge the lump that had formed. "I appreciate the information, though."

Darrel nodded and walked away. "Sorry man."

"Damn." His brother-in-law sighed and flagged

over the events coordinator, Becca. "Hey, Bec, can you watch my table for a few minutes? I've got to see Lena and Jag needs to go see his woman."

"Sure." Becca breezed past them to take her place behind Alex's table.

"Be back in ten, okay?" Alex assured her.

They headed toward Sawyer's table.

"She's not my..." Jagger didn't finish because she was his woman, damn it. Always had been. Sure, he'd dated some, but no one ever compared. Now all he had to do was continue to show her how much she meant to him and let her know that's the way it was going to be. He smiled and Alex snickered.

"Yeah, that's what I thought," he said. It hadn't taken but another minute to get there.

The boys were smitten and Lena seemed amused. "I swear, I can't remember the last time they sat this long. It's going on ten minutes."

"Uh oh, Jag. Looks like you might have some competition," Alex teased as he watched his boys blush and squirm in their seats.

Sawyer looked cute while she worked her magic drawing their portraits.

Lena giggled, Alex wrapped his arms around her, and Jagger winked at Sawyer. "I see that."

"Almost finished. You guys are doing great," Sawyer said. He knew she was biting her lip to keep from laughing. "There."

She ripped the large piece of paper off her art pad and turned it around to show them the finished product. It was remarkable. The shading and hand-drawn details made the boys pop from the page. It was like looking at a black and white replica of

Corbin and Carter in the flesh. It was incredible.

"Wow." Lena gasped. "Would you look at that, Alex?"

"I see." His brother-in-law gushed. "If the tattooing thing doesn't work out, I may know a few people with galleries who might be interested in your work." He said. Jagger knew he was being serious too.

"Let me see."

"No. I wanna see," The boys said, so she showed it to them too.

"Cool!" They said in unison. A cart filled with candy apples passed by and that caught their attention. "Can we have one of those?"

"Not before dinner," Alex answered sternly, and Corbin and Carter whined.

"Aw, no fair."

Lena tipped Sawyer handsomely. "This is being framed before we leave here today. Thank you. It was so good to see you again."

"Anytime." Sawyer smiled and ruffled the kids' hair. "You all take it easy on your parents, you hear?"

"Oh, they will," Alex said. "Won't you, boys?"

"Yes, daddy."

"Good," Alex replied, extending his hand to shake hers. "Welcome back, Sawyer. It's good to see you again, and my condolences to you on your sister's passing. Carley was a good woman." She could only nod before he turned to address Jagger. "Jag, we will see you around, most definitely." He nodded and guided his family away to give them space. The minute Alex had mentioned her sister, Sawyer had gasped as if shocked that they had found out what happened and with wide eyes, she looked in his direction before she masked her reaction.

The cat was out of the bag now, baby, and he was for damn sure not going to let her go through it alone. She'd see soon enough.

***

Sawyer

Becca had done an amazing job of organizing the art fair. The Kerrville Arts Centre was packed and Sawyer was in awe of the participation for such an event. There were locals all over the place. Although the Arts Centre was open to the public, the tables were mostly set up outside of the beautiful historical building and she appreciated that. It was such a beautiful day.

"Welcome to the KAC. So what do you think?" Becca asked as she gestured to the space around them.

"I think I don't know how you find the time." Sawyer smiled. "It's great, Becca. Thank you for including me in this."

Becca Everett was a busy woman and clearly remarkable when it came to managing her time. She owned several commercial properties, was very active in the community, which included being on the board of directors for the KAC, and to top it off, had to take care of and raise her younger brother when their parents died in a car crash. Sawyer was exhausted just thinking of it.

"I've always been a sucker for art." Becca

winked. "I even paint in my spare time. Not that I'd be courageous enough to show anyone." She picked up one of Mad Ink's business cards and pocketed it. "Glad you could make it, though. We've got clay pottery, bronze sculptures, portraits, paintings, handmade jewelry, author tables, and the exhibits inside to check out…you name it. So, have fun when you get the chance and if you need anything, I'll be around."

"Okay, now, this I've got to see. You paint? That's awesome. Maybe I'll have to get you to make me something for the shop." Sawyer was being serious, but Becca brushed it off.

"If you say so. Look, I've got to get back to it but if you need anything, like I said I won't be too far away."

"Sure, see ya." Sawyer waved as Becca departed and after she finished setting up, she sat down to sketch while she waited. The Mad Ink banner was up, her portfolios were out, her cards were available for anyone to help themselves, and the sketch pad was in her hands. For the first time in a long time, she felt like she was in her element again.

A few hours into it and several portraits later, the hair on the back of her neck stood up. But it wasn't a cool breeze that had caused this reaction. It was the man himself. This happened to her every single time and it was better than she remembered.

Jagger.

Anytime he was within reach, she could tell. The energy around her seemed to change and she could feel the magnetism between the two of them sizzle like electricity. She bit her lip and admired him from afar. He was standing at one of the tables with one of his older sisters. If her memory served correctly, it was Lena. He stood with whom she assumed was his brother-in-law and both men laughed at the two kids' shenanigans, which made Sawyer smile too. They were adorable. She was pretty sure Alex and Lena were high school sweethearts too, a few years older, and had known Carley better than they'd known Sawyer.

Just then, a young couple stopped by her table and began to browse her portfolio, so she put a stop to her thoughts and approached them. "Hey, there. Are you thinking of getting some work done?"

"Yeah. We're getting married and we were thinking of getting something on our fingers instead of the traditional rings, so we're looking around," The man said.

"Well, you've stopped by the right place. Mad Ink opens up the week after next." Sawyer handed them her business card and smiled again. "Feel free to keep on browsing, and when you're ready, give us a call and we'll make you an appointment."

"Thanks!" The man pocketed it and she left them alone.

"You started it."

"No, you did." The two adorable boys began to shove each other until their mother stepped in.

"You boys better behave, or so help me, you will not be going horseback riding with Gramps later. You'll also have to go to bed early and you won't be going on that campout with your friend Travis next week, either. You hear?"

"Yes, momma." The boys stilled and the woman's

stern facial expression melted like butter. She winked at Sawyer and introduced herself.

"Hey, there. I'm not sure if you remember me. I'm Lena Dean, formerly Hale, and these are my sons Corbin and Carter. Jagger pointed you out and I was wondering if you could draw the boys, if they'll sit still long enough. I've always wanted something unique to put on top of the mantle."

"Absolutely." Sawyer giggled at the two miniature Deans' pouting expressions and extended her hand. "My name is Sawyer. It's a pleasure to meet you." After shaking Lena's hand, she bent to address the boys. "Sure looks like you both have a lot to look forward to, from what I heard. Horseback riding and a campout? What very lucky boys you are. Now, if I promise to be as quick as I can with your momma's request, do you think you can handle sitting down to pose for me?"

They eyed her skeptically as she led them to a chair behind her table. She whispered, "We good?"

"Yes, ma'am."

She'd been drawing for so long, it felt like she could do this in her sleep. Lena's boys were angels and it took her maybe ten or fifteen minutes to finish their drawings. In the meantime, Jagger and Alex swaggered over and her heart pounded double time.

Sawyer did her best to keep focus on the task at hand while Lena, Alex, and Jagger bantered with one another. She sighed with longing as it made her think of her own sister and how much she was dearly missed. It also reminded Sawyer of how utterly lonely she was most of the time.

It gets better Sawyer. It has to. At least, that's

what people say. Just breathe.

She plastered on a smile to hide her inner turmoil.

"Almost finished up. You guys are doing great," Sawyer said. "There."

She ripped the large piece of paper off her art pad and turned it around to show them all the finished product.

"Wow," Lena gasped. "Would you look at that, Alex?"

"I see," Alex gushed. "If the tattooing thing doesn't work out, I may know a few people with galleries who might be interested in your work."

Sawyer was speechless. She watched as the boys argued about which of them could see it first. It was adorable.

"Cool!" They said in unison when she showed them their cute little faces on paper. A second later a cart filled with candy apples passed by and that caught their attention. "Can we have one of those?"

The boys whined while Sawyer graciously accepted the tip Lena insisted on.

"This is being framed before we leave here today. Thank you."

"Anytime." Sawyer smiled and ruffled the kids' hair. "You all take it easy on your parents, you hear?"

"Oh, they will," Alex said. "Won't you boys?"

"Yes, daddy."

"Good," Alex replied. He then extended his hand towards her to shake hers. "Welcome back, Sawyer. It's good to see you again. My condolences to you on your sister's passing. Carley was a good woman." She could only nod before he turned to address Jagger. "Jag we will see you around most definitely."

She watched Jagger nod his head as Alex led his family away and she tried to mask her shock that Alex recognized her, let alone found out about her sister's tragic passing.

You will not cry here, you will not...

"You're stronger than you realize," Jagger said as if he'd read her mind. He stepped closer. "I'm so sorry about Carley, baby." He hugged her and she had to wipe the tears from her eyes.

Dang it!

"I can't talk about this here, Jag. I'll be a mess," she confessed.

"Understood. But have dinner with me. We can talk about whatever you want later. I just miss you," he said as he tilted her chin, so he could kiss her on the forehead.

Sawyer could see the complete sincerity of his words on his face because he looked at her like she was his everything right then and she gasped. "You sure about that? I've always had so much baggage, Jag. You deserve better than me."

"The hell I do. You're an amazing woman. When are you going to realize it? Because I'm telling you now, I want to be the man who shows you. Have dinner with me. Stop running."

"I don't know." Sawyer stepped away from him because it was hard to think when he was touching her. Was she ready to put herself out there again? To love him and risk being hurt once more? She'd already lost everything once and the one person she could always count on was now dead. She was scared to take the risk.

Her heart battled with her mind. The latter was

telling her to stay cautious, while deep down, she already knew it was too late because the other night with him had solidified it. She was already in love. He was her one and only. She sighed. "Fine. Pick me up tomorrow at seven?"

"You won't regret this, sugar." Jagger exhaled, giving her an electrifying smile. "You'll see."

Chapter Five

Sawyer

Sawyer hoped she wasn't trying too hard. It'd taken her almost all afternoon to get herself ready for their date tonight and she'd dressed up instead of sticking to her preferred jeans and tee look. Why was she feeling so nervous now?

It's Jag, Sawyer. He's seen you at your worst and still wanted you, remember?

Sawyer sighed as she stood in front of the floor-length mirror to look at herself one last time. Her hair cascaded in loose waves down her shoulders and back. She'd taken her time to curl it and it added a touch of volume to her already thick locks. As for makeup, she went with a smoky eye look and bright red lips to match her outfit. It put a new definition to the little black dress, short, tight, and sleeveless, to show off her tattoos and curvy figure. She completed it all with a pair of cute red fuck-me-pumps and she was feeling badass now.

Here goes nothin'.

She blew herself a kiss as the doorbell rang.

"Hello, cowboy." She opened the door to Jagger and leaned against the frame while she checked him out. "Look at you all gussied up and looking good."

His dark brown hair couldn't be tamed. It was messy, but sexy on him, and it curled a little around the nape of his neck. He wore a form-fitting dark blue button-down that accentuated his fit body and she wanted to drool. Instead, she cleared her throat.

"Says the woman who looks good enough to eat." His gaze intensified and ignited with passion, as if he'd like to skip dinner all together and head straight to a Sawyer-flavored dessert.

"Why, Jag, I'm flattered." She fluttered her eyes at him and chuckled. "I'll just grab my purse and I'm ready to hit the road." There was a little more bounce in her step and sway in her hips as she went to get it. "I need sustenance first and we can talk dessert later on." She winked at him and he groaned.

"Woman, you test my patience. Now get that sweet butt into the truck so I can show you off. I'll be the envy of any man who sees you because tonight you're mine, sugar. And Sawyer, you can count on making those arrangements because I plan on loving you long and hard honey. Long and hard." He tapped her ass on the way out of the house and chuckled when she squealed with delight.

They were on their way.

"So where are you taking me, anyway?" Sawyer smoothed her hands down her short skirt and fidgeted in the truck. That little tap on the butt along with his promising words made her hot and bothered, so the subject change was welcome because she desperately needed to take her mind off thinking about all the deliciousness that was Jagger and the things he'd do to her.

"I'm bringing you to the Steak House and figured we could stop by for a drink at Tipsy's after." Jagger shrugged. "That okay?"

"Hell yeah!" She grinned. "I love steak. Miss me some good ol' barbeque. The drink sounds good too, but could we make a stop first after we eat?"

He nodded and lifted a brow as he took a quick peek at her before looking back at the road ahead of them. "What'd you have in mind?"

"My livelihood," she said, facing him enthusiastically. "Mad Ink is opening in a few days and I wanted to show you its progress. It's amazing, Jag. My dream is coming true. I never thought I'd make it happen in Kerrville, of all places, considering my past but now..." She reached for his hand and gave it a squeeze before letting go. "Now, there's no other place I'd rather be."

"I love hearing that." He glanced at her again and gulped. "I'm proud of you, Sawyer. Always have been. I'm truly sorry for what happened to Carley. I know she'd be proud too. You're not alone anymore, sweetheart, and I thank God every day that we've been given this second chance to get to know each other again because honestly, there's no place I'd rather be, either."

"Wow," she whispered, completely in awe with him. He always managed to find a way to take her breath away. "You sure have a way with words. Thank you!" She blinked a couple of times to fight back her happy tears and the moment he stopped the truck in the restaurant parking lot, she flung herself into his arms to show him her appreciation with a kiss.

His soft, plump lips were delectable and molded against hers like they were meant to be there. She slipped her tongue inside them and caressed it against his. He hoisted her onto his lap to get more comfortable, but they took their time exploring each other. They kept it appropriate for the public, yet neither were in a rush to leave the warm truck now. Sawyer reveled in his taste. She was totally hooked. His hard body pressed tightly to hers and her nipples puckered, her pussy flooded, and she ached in the most delicious way possible before he pulled away breathlessly.

"Well, you have an amazing way of showing your appreciation." He smiled and gripped her hips tighter. "We've got to slow down, sugar, because I'm right near my breaking point. Let's get you some grub, fuel you up, and get on with our night. There'll be plenty more where that came from." He winked and reluctantly lifted her off, so he could open his door.

"Promise?" She touched her lips where she could still feel him and waited for him to open her door.

"Now, have I ever let you down?"

Sawyer stayed silent for a minute because old insecurities came to surface from so long ago. Jagger took notice.

"Hey, you okay?" He tilted her chin with his finger, so she couldn't avoid his gaze.

"Yes and no." She smiled shyly, hating, yet loving

how well he knew her cues. "What I mean is, I'm fine. And no, you haven't let me down yet."

"Good," he said, giving her a quick peck on the cheek. "Now, let's eat."

The Steak House was a busy barbeque joint and a cozy family restaurant. The smell of mesquite steaks, burgers, and chicken fried steak assaulted her senses when they walked in. Her mouth watered and her stomach growled in anticipation. Man, she was hungry now for something other than the man she was with.

She giggled as they took their seats.

"What's so funny?" Jagger became immediately intrigued.

"My tummy's rumbling, my mouth is watering, the smell in here is divine, and I can't wait to dig in." Sawyer shrugged. "Before we arrived, the only delectable thing I wanted to take a big ol' bite out of was you. Now that we're in here, I'm hungry for the food."

"Fair enough." He chuckled. "How about we order?"

He flagged the waitress over and they ordered beer and appetizers while they waited for the main course. Jagger ordered a ribeye, rare, with all the fixings and she went with a sirloin, medium, with a side of rice.

They sat in comfortable silence while Sawyer checked out the rest of the restaurant. Wooden floors, paneled walls, and cowboy memorabilia as far as the eye could see surrounded them. There was a small bar on the left and a couple of big screens above it. Their waitress came back with their potato skins and whatever was on tap and when she left, Sawyer felt the need to apologize. "Hey, Jag, about the other night…"

"What about it?" He grabbed the appetizer and took a big bite while hers remained on the plate.

"I'm sorry for running. When I was on the phone with Toby, it brought a lot of stuff up, you know, about Carley." She paused for a second and took a deep breath. "I miss her something fierce. Toby's taking it just as hard, if not worse. Anyway, then I got the roses. That combined with all your other sweet gestures got me thinking about us and what we had. I didn't want to be alone and, well, I must be honest with you. My intention was for you to make me feel good, you know, to forget even if for only a little while, and believe me you did. It was the feelings it brought up after we did the deed that scared the crap out of me and I needed some time to sort it out."

"So, you used me for sex." Jagger lifted a brow and she could see he tried to keep a straight face but couldn't. "Trust me, sugar. I do not mind, not at all."

"Thank God," she said with a deep breath. She felt a little better now that she opened up. She started to eat too but nearly choked when he continued to talk.

"I still think I should make my intentions clear before we go on. I'm not into games, Sawyer. We're both too old for that and your feelings aren't one-sided. When I'm with you, I want more. Hell, I want it all. We can go as fast or as slow as you need, but I can't let you go again. Tell me you're okay with that."

"Um…" Her eyes widened in shock and she was

utterly speechless. She needed a second to process what he was asking. "Y-you want to be exclusive?"

The look on his face told her all she needed to know because he was giving her a "well, duh" expression. "You're damn right I do. You've always been mine, Sawyer, and from the moment I realized it was really you and you were back for good, I also knew I never stopped loving you."

"Wow, there you go again. How is it you can easily take my breath away every time we're together?" She asked with a wide smile.

But Jagger groaned. "Would you please put me out of my misery, woman, and answer the question?"

"Which one was that again?" She teased, but when his eyes narrowed, she surrendered. "Okay, okay, I'm sorry. The answer to your question is I think I am. I love you too, Jag. But are you sure you're ready for my kind of messed up? My sister just died, I'm on my own, and I'm busy with starting the business."

"You should know by now that your kind of crazy doesn't scare me, sugar. You're not alone anymore and if I have my way, you never will be again. We clear?"

"Crystal." She snickered. "Just wanted you to know what you are getting yourself into. I haven't had a relationship since you. I hope I remember how."

"Now I'm speechless," he teased. "Not one guy since me?"

"Oh, there were guys, but nothing serious." She shrugged and there was a visible tick in Jagger's cheek as he thought about it.

"You don't say," he growled. She reached across the table to hold his hand.

"There was only one you, Jag. I think you ruined me for all other men, so breathe, baby. It's all good. Besides, it's not like I was your only." She challenged.

He took a deep breath.

"You were the one that mattered most," he replied.

"Nice save." Sawyer laughed. "See? All is good." The waitress set down their entrees and when she left, Sawyer continued. "Now let's just leave the past where it belongs and enjoy our moments from now on. I'm having a good time tonight."

"Me too," he grunted as he cut his steak. "So, I ruined you for all men, huh?"

"I knew you'd like that bit of information." She shook her head, completely amused.

"It's good for the ego." He smirked and took a big bite of steak with gusto.

"Oh, hush up and eat," she said, still amused with him. They went back to their comfortable silence during the meal. Twenty-five minutes later, they were sipping coffee and waiting for the check when their bubble of happiness burst.

"Well, well, well. Look what the cat dragged in." Stacey sneered. "Sewer Maddox."

Sawyer stiffened, and her face was void of emotion while she replied. "Stacey, we're not kids anymore and you're about as welcome as a wet shoe so move along." She faced Jagger again to dismiss the other woman, hoping she'd take the hint and move on, but there was no such luck. One of her past tormentors was right there in the flesh and by the looks of it, she was just getting started.

"I heard you were back in town and I couldn't believe my ears." She looked at Sawyer as if she was scum stuck to the bottom of a barrel. Jagger's face turned red with anger. "Imagine my surprise when I walk in here and see Jagger slumming it again with Kerrville's trashiest."

"Careful there, Stacey. You're showing the horns holding up that halo you pretend to have." Jagger stood before Sawyer could stop him. She didn't need him to fight her battles for her anymore. She wasn't the timid little girl she had once been. She was a grown woman with a big heart and thick skin. She wasn't afraid of a little blonde stick figure talking smack. She wouldn't go back there again.

"Whatever, Hale. Look at you both. She's some kind of rock wannabe and you're all country. The two don't go together," Stacey spat.

"That is the stupidest thing I've ever heard. There's more to people than appearances, Stacey, and I feel sorry for you, if you haven't realized that already. So what? I have tattoos and a few piercings. It makes me interesting and an individual. I don't want to be cookie cutter, but if that's your thing, more power to you. I don't know what it is I did to make you hate me, but you need to get over it and move on with your life." Sawyer was getting exasperated with the situation and people were staring. She was done giving this woman power over her self-esteem and decided to take the higher road by talking it out instead of getting hot-headed about the insults.

But Stacey didn't take the hint. She seemed to get angrier the more they didn't give her the reaction she expected and there was only so much a woman could take. Some people were just born mean.

"I heard about the fire." She feigned a pout at Sawyer while her eyes narrowed. "Poor, poor maggot."

Okay it is on, make fun of me all you want but you do not, and I repeat do not say anything about the people I love. Carley had sacrificed so much for her and the moment she heard the disrespect coming out of Stacey's mouth by calling her sister that deplorable name like she'd done as they were kids, Sawyer was out of her chair so fast and in Stacey's face in an instant. Sawyer talked low and pretended to smile as onlookers gawked but the warning was obvious in her tone.

"I'd like to remind you that we're not kids anymore and in case you haven't noticed, I'm not the same person I once was. I'm no pushover, so think twice before anything else comes out of that filthy little mouth. You're going to leave me alone, you're going to leave Jagger alone, and if you ever, and I mean ever say anything bad about my sister again, I will end you. You got me?"

"Um hum," she squeaked. "Whatever."

"Good. Now move along and remember what I said." Sawyer took a deep breath when she sat down again. She gave Stacey one last glare and the other woman bolted for the door. Man, she hated confrontation, but she hated feeling inferior even more. That part of her past was behind her.

"Dang, you're sexy." Jagger shook his head in

awe. "Remind me to stay on your good side."

***

"So, this is it," Sawyer said as she fished the keys out of her purse to let them inside the tattoo shop. "They installed the sign this morning. What do you think?" She gestured towards the front window. She wasn't as enthusiastic to show him her shop as she had been earlier. Her confrontation with Stacey lingered and it bothered her to know that the horrible woman was affecting her yet again.

The sign was simple, yet still stood out in the crowd of the other retail shops around. It took up most of the space on her window and lit up in the background. She'd come up with the design herself and special ordered it from a drawing she'd composed. Black ink dripped from a hand holding a gun in the top left corner. Bold, dark lettering followed it with the store's name and at the bottom, there were two blue butterflies which represented Carley and Sawyer's last memory together. It seemed like a lifetime ago now.

"Looks good," he grunted. "I like it." Jagger stepped up behind her and rubbed the tension out of her shoulders while she opened the door. It was as if he could sense her strain and she already felt a little better, thanks to him.

Sawyer turned the lights on, relocked the door behind them, and watched him quietly while he took it all in. The interior was nice and bright with a ton of recessed lighting and it was so much better than the fluorescent crap most places used. She chose a simple eggshell white for the walls except for the big one in the back where she had just finished up her mural. Splashes and streaks of color were chosen to give the impression that paint was being used on a canvas in the background. It was a watercolor effect combined with a little realism to make it pop. Sawyer painted a nature piece that consisted of a beautiful forest background with fairies in it. They both stood in the lounge at the front still. There were oversized, red leather guest chairs with a couple of glass tables in front, a coffee machine near the black reception counter, and her portfolios lined a couple of the shelves on a bookcase on the other side.

Sawyer sighed and set her purse on one of the seats.

"There are two tattoo rooms in the back, a small office, as well as a spot for piercing. If all goes as planned, Mace should be here in a couple of days ready to start." She shrugged and moved further into the space. "So…"

Jagger stood there motionless and Sawyer fidgeted as she waited for his reaction.

He smiled.

"You're telling me that I take your breath away. Well, woman, you do the same to me." He swaggered forward and met her behind the counter. Sawyer sagged against it and hunched her shoulders in relief.

"You sure about that? I'm rock and you're all country remember? We can't possibly work." She made a funny face and he just shook his head at her.

"Oh, we work, babe. I'm sure anyone who told you otherwise is a stupid bitch," he said, referring to Stacey. "So get any bad thoughts out of that pretty little head because you were mine the moment our eyes connected in high school and I finally convinced you to take a chance on me. Things might have been a little fucked up for a while and it made us lose our way, but now that I've got you again, you can be damn sure I'm going to remind you every single day how special you are." His body was now flush against hers. He kissed her forehead and his lips trailed down to her ear and he whispered the rest. It gave her goose bumps. "So here I am, a man telling his woman she takes his breath away because I love you, and every day that goes by, you not only intrigue me, but you inspire me to be a better person. You work hard, you're making your dreams a reality, and this place is so fucking beautiful, it's a work of art, just like its owner."

"Well, there you go again," she said. Her heart beat faster, her palms turned sweaty, and she fisted his shirt to hold on to him tighter, "being all sweet."

"Who's Mace and should I be worried?" Jagger leaned back a little and arched a brow at her as she laughed at him. It took her a minute to compose herself enough to answer.

"Hell, no!" she said, wiping her eyes. She laughed so hard she was crying. "Mace is like an annoying cousin, but a great friend. He worked in Toby's shop but he's been looking for a change ever since the fire remodel began, so he's coming my way to help me out here. He's a fantastic tattooist and it would be nice to work with someone familiar."

"Good," he grunted.

"I kind of like it when you get all jealous on me," she teased, letting out one last fit of giggles at his expense until he quieted her down with one hell of a kiss. Jagger sucked on her bottom lip hard before he gave her no choice but to open for him. He probed her mouth with his tongue and he loved her mouth like she wanted him to love her pussy right then. This man had oodles of talent when it came to playing with her body. Sawyer writhed against him and groaned. "J-Jag, baby I really like where this is heading, I do, but um…" He was so hungry for her, she had to talk through his kisses as he devoured her between her lips and neck. "Not here. Let's christen the office."

The number one rule was to keep the place as clean and sanitary as possible, so that meant no dirty business or sex of any kind in any areas there might be clients or equipment. Her office, however, was game on. It was her territory and there was no way she was waiting any longer to get a good taste of her man. Besides, she had a couch they could make use of. Round one was a go.

Without a word, Jagger lifted her off of her feet, so she had no choice but to wrap her legs around his waist. Her short skirt lifted to her hips and he grabbed her bare ass and squeezed. "In the back, third door on the left." She exhaled and claimed his mouth again. She needed him more than she wanted her next breath. There was no coming up for air. Her pussy had already soaked her thong and she only got wetter when she rubbed her mound against his thick hard cock, still confined behind the fly of his jeans. "Mm."

Their kiss became nothing but tongue and teeth and this had to be the best dessert she'd ever tasted. She thought of his dick now and what it would be like to have it in her mouth. Oral sex made her feel empowered when she was the one giving it, and she hadn't had the pleasure of experiencing that with him yet. Boy, did she want to, though.

Jagger fumbled with the doorknob before it finally clicked open, and he kicked the door shut again behind them. It was then she came up for air and it took a few seconds for her to catch her breath. "Will you strip for me?"

"You really have to ask?" He ever so slowly lowered her to the ground. He went to reach for her, but Sawyer wagged her finger at him and stepped back.

"Uh, uh, uh," she mumbled. "I want to enjoy the show first."

Jagger rolled his eyes at her but complied. He quickly fisted his shirt and lifted it over his head before he threw it in the corner. Next, he toed off his boots, kicked them aside, and removed his socks. He wasted no time loosening his belt, undoing his buckle, and lowering his zipper before shimmying out of his pants. Next came his boxer briefs and he kicked them aside as well and stood buck naked.

"You're a masterpiece, Jag," Sawyer remarked. *Hot damn!* She was about ready to combust. "I need to enjoy the view for a minute. Stay still, will you? I promise to make it worth your while."

He grunted while hands fisted at his sides and she could tell it took him some effort to let her come close without touching her right back. "That first night at Tipsy's, I remember you telling me you had some ink on our way to my car, but I have yet to see it." She arched a brow as she slowly circled his body.

"The last time we made love, we were in such a heated rush, I don't even think you got fully naked. So I missed it then, but now I wanna see."

There was a tick in his jaw as she took her sweet time taking him all in. She circled around to his back and stopped because there it was, right there on the back of his right calf. A tattoo of a football helmet with his old jersey number on the side of it. But it was the other detail that had her gasping because hanging from it was a charm shaped like a heart with the letter S inside. She was pretty sure what that stood for but didn't want to make assumptions until he was ready to share its story with her. So instead, she kept quiet and moved until she stood in front of him again. "It's beautiful, Jagger."

Sawyer dropped to her knees before he could say anything. Face to cock now, he was so aroused pre-cum glistened from the head. She lapped it up and the moment the salty taste hit her tongue, she wanted to savor him. One hand lifted and spread on his torso to push him back against the wall behind them. His hands tangled inside her hair and he guided her movements just the way he liked. His cock hit the back of her throat repeatedly, slowly at first and then his hips flexed faster. She gripped the base of his cock with her hand and moved it along in rhythm with her mouth. Her other hand played with his balls now, testing their weight and fondling them. Jagger panted, she sucked harder, and moved her tongue along as best as she could to taste every delectable inch. She could tell he was close when his grip on her tightened, his eyes squinted shut, and he cursed. "Pull back, sugar. I'm about to blow."

She squirmed as her own clit pulsed with achy need, but it was his turn to come first for a change. She ignored his warning and kept right on sucking his cock with enthusiasm. It seemed like every sense heightened when feelings were involved, and she wanted to feel him erupt all the way down her throat. She gripped his ass and encouraged him to fuck her face some more. His legs shook, his pecker twitched, and he threw his head back in bliss, moaning her name out loud while he unloaded his thick creamy essence in her mouth.

He sagged to the floor to catch his breath when it was all said and done, and she loved the sight of him there in her space. Her heart soared and for the first time in a long time she began to have hope again. Then it clicked.

"I'm done chasing," she said, surprising herself when she'd blurted it out.

Jagger opened his eyes and smirked at her. "What was that?"

She shrugged. "Carley's last wish for me was to go chasing butterflies and it just hit me that the chase is done, thanks to you."

"I still don't quite understand." He shook his head as he got to his feet and held out his hand, so he could help her up from the ground as well. "You have way too many clothes on, by the way." He winked as he reached behind her to undo her zipper. "Care to explain?"

"She once told me that even after many years together with Toby, she could still feel the excitement in her belly every time he was near. She wanted that for me with my own relationship, wanted

70

me to settle down and…"

"Get those butterflies," Jagger interrupted. "And, you got them with me?" He smiled again and his chest puffed out.

"I do," Sawyer agreed. "You're the one."

"You're damn right I am." He kissed her quickly as her dress hit the floor. She stepped out of it and rolled her eyes. He made smug look sexy at the moment and it kind of annoyed her that she didn't care one bit. It was the truth.

"Oh, shut up and love me already, would you?"

"Thought you'd never ask." He walked her backwards and wiggled his eyebrows. "It's your turn now, but first…" He pushed her down on the couch and she squealed as she fell backwards onto the plush cushions. He knelt down, gripped the sides of her underwear and pulled them off. "I need you to know you do the same for me, Sawyer. I love you, sugar, and I will from now until eternity." Her eyes glistened as he spread her legs wide and she bit her lip as he admired her shiny pussy spread before him. He dove right in licking her from ass to clit in one smooth motion. She gripped his head and arched her back in response.

"Oh, God, this is not going to last, Jag." Sawyer shook already and he was just getting started.

"It's a good thing I have enough stamina for the both of us, then." He looked slightly amused when he went back to feast. This time he went agonizingly slow by licking her outer lips and then sucking on each. He tongued her opening next and pumped it in and out like he did with his cock and she needed more. Sucking his dick had worked her up and she needed to come and then feel him filling her, joined as one.

"Please," she begged. The grip on his hair got tighter and she thrust her pussy closer, guiding his face to where she needed him most of all.

Like the amazing man she knew he was, he obliged her request and concentrated on her clit with gusto. Jagger was like a starving man in need of sustenance now. He licked, flicked, sucked, and nibbled until her body convulsed and she screamed out his name in ecstasy. Her nipples puckered, her body tingled, and her eyes rolled to the back of her head before she came back to her senses again. It took only about a minute for him to get a condom on and he was back on top of her, thrusting inside. She was so wet, there was no resistance and she moved with him, so he could be as deep as possible. "Fuck me like you own it, baby. Make me yours and claim this cunt," she growled.

Her head hit the arm rest on the couch they were on and he pounded into her harder like she requested. He left no doubt who she belonged to and she loved everything about it. "Mine," he grunted, as he kissed her as hard as he fucked her. It was heaven.

He pulled all the way out and rubbed against her clit as he filled her pussy repeatedly and within five minutes tops, her body ignited for a second time. Her scream was unintelligible, her pussy pulsed, and she came so hard she could feel herself squirt around him so much so that she'd made as much of a mess as he had when he filled the condom inside of her. It was literally the best sex she'd ever had.

Later, after they'd cleaned themselves up, she lay

in his arms and mentioned the tattoo on his leg. "Does it remind you of the glory days?"

"Does what?" He asked, rubbing her back.

"The tattoo on your leg. I have a feeling it has meaning, so what's the story there?"

"It's like you said." He shrugged. "It's a reminder of a better time in my life. I got it about a year after you left and I had the tattoo designed to represent the two loves of my life. One is football and my love for playing the game at the time, and the other is my heart with the initial of the only woman I've ever loved." He gulped as Sawyer adjusted herself so that she was sitting on top of him. "I knew you were one of a kind, way before you left me and I knew I'd probably never be lucky enough to have what we had ever again. You're it for me babe, and it was a constant reminder to never forget."

"That's the most beautiful thing anyone has ever said to me." Sawyer touched her heart and wiped away a happy tear. "I'd say that I'm the lucky one though, because here we are together again. The longing is finally gone and I feel whole when we're together. You're stuck with me, Jagger.

"Thank fuck," he growled, slid his hand behind her head, and urged her forward so he could kiss the shit out of her. "Spend the night."

He let go of her so she could sit up. Sawyer looked around her office and giggled. "Not here, I hope."

"The next time I take you, I want you in my bed. We've been together in my barn and now in your office. I want someplace comfortable where I can fall asleep with you in my arms afterward and still have you there in the morning. Agreed?"

73

"Agreed." Sawyer nodded.

"Good. Now, get dressed so we can hit the road." Jagger tapped her butt to get her moving and once they were both dressed, he opened the door for her only to stop her half way through. He caressed the side of her face with his hand and took a minute to really look at her.

"You okay?" She asked curiously. His penetrating gaze sizzled and she could see the love he held for her there. He had completely opened up and it left her with no doubt in her mind when he finally answered her.

"Never better. I plan to show you that every single day from this moment on."

"Sounds like a plan to me," she said, holding his hand as she led the way out the door. Now that there were no misunderstandings between them, they accepted their second chance and were ready to move forward, it was smooth sailing to their happily ever after.

It took a while to learn that anything is possible if you're willing to take a leap, and she had to work through all of her problems to finally accept that. Distance was their true test of love and Jagger gave her the ability to smile for no reason at all.

Life was good.

Epilogue

Mace

The self-serve gas station was deserted as he filled up his motorcycle except for the attendant behind the counter inside waiting for him to pay up. Fuck, it was hot, and all he wanted was some food, a shower, and a comfortable bed to catch some Z's. It'd been a long trip but well worth the headache to get here. Sawyer was like a sister to all of them and Toby had sent him up here to keep an eye on things. They worried about her up here all alone with so many bad memories to keep her company.

He needed a change of scenery and this was his chance to start over.

He was done pumping and tightened his gas cap before he ran inside to get a move on. Baby Girl was waiting for him and would probably be worried if he didn't show up soon. He straddled the bike, unhooked his helmet and was about to put it on when a noise from across the street distracted him from his task.

The woman making the racket was short, stacked, and curvy in all the right places. Not his usual type, but she intrigued him none the less, even from afar, so he thought, *what the hell* and ran across the street to see what the matter was.

The woman was on the sidewalk in front of the store she'd just left and was quickly scrambling to get all her stuff back inside the sack she'd dropped by accident. "Can I help you out over here?" He knelt to get a better look at her haggard state. She was anxious about something, but what? It hadn't taken long to find out once he paid better attention to the situation.

"I'm such a klutz sometimes, I swear," she mumbled, finally looking up. "If you'd really like to help, you'll pass me my belongings before that old coot comes over. She's a gossip and I don't need the headache."

He looked behind him were she pointed to see a wrinkly old lady about two blocks away approaching fast. "Whatever you say," he said with a shrug. He quickly helped her out, only to realize why she was so frantic as he was putting everything he'd found back in the bag she held out. She looked innocent, but she was anything but. He arched a brow up in surprise to see a monstrous pink vibrator, some anal lube, and various other sex toys inside. He shifted when his dick got hard and nearly groaned. Clearly his cock had plans of his own.

"Brodie Mace, but my friends just call me Mace. And you are?" He held out his hand as he introduced himself and waited for her to do the same.

Her face flushed and she quickly stuffed the bag back in her oversized purse to hide the evidence of what he saw inside, but little did she know he had a photographic memory. Oh, this woman was something, all right. Someone he wouldn't mind getting to know better. Innocent on the outside, but clearly something wild in the sheets.

His kind of woman, after all.

"Oh, I'm Becca. Becca Everett." She finally shook his hand just as the little old lady caught up to them.

"I saw you dropped the bags, dear, and I rushed right over to make sure you were all right."

The nosey little bitty eyed him up and he sighed. "Brodie Mace, a pleasure to meet you, Ma'am." He shook her hand too and he could feel Becca's eyes studying him, so he looked at her. "From what I could tell, it was all an accident, but Becca here is fine and all of her stuff has been accounted for." He smiled when she blushed, a deeper red this time. He decided to save her yet again. "Well, I'm running late so I've got to get going." He addressed the old woman. "Would you like some help crossing the street?" He didn't have a clue where she was headed but held out his arm for her to accept.

When she did, Becca looked relieved. "See you around, Becca," he said, and he meant it. She was such a conundrum and it piqued his curiosity. Plus, she kind of owed him one and he was hoping to cash in with dinner sometime or something.

"Oh, thank you, dear." The old lady patted his arm once they were across and he quickly bid her adieu without even getting her name.

Soon, he was on the road again, helmet on his head, sunglasses shading his eyes, and the rumble of his motorcycle vibrating on his ass. He was on his way and the new scenery already held promise.

Ten minutes later, Sawyer was running out of her house as he shut down the bike. She hugged him something fierce as soon as she could and he laughed while he hugged her back. It was so good to see her again and looking so happy too. It was a pleasant surprise. "How you doing, squirt?"

"Ha, ha," she said, flipping him the bird. "It's good to see you, Mace. Took you long enough."

"Tell me about it," he teased. "I need food, a good wash, and some sleep. But before any of that, I need you to tell me more about the lovely Becca Everett. Know her?"

Sawyer smiled, her eyes lit up, and she rubbed her hands together. He knew that look because she'd given it to him the last time she tried to set him up with someone. Only this time he didn't mind. Not one bit.

***

If you enjoyed reading *Chasing Butterflies*, stay tuned for Mace and Becca's story, *Cowgirl Crazy*. Toby James' story is in progress, as well, in *Forever with You, The Misfit Tattoo Series*. Enjoy!

***

Also, don't forget to consider leaving a review.

It's greatly appreciated.
Thank you!

About the Author

Jennifer Labelle resides in Canada with her husband and three beautiful children. After her third child she became a stay at home mom. In her busy household Jennifer likes to spend her down time engrossed in the stories that she creates. She is an active reader of romance, mystery and anything paranormal. With an education in Addictions work she's decided to take a less stressful approach in life and hopes that you enjoy, as she shares some of her imagination and artistic inspiration with all of you.

Facebook:
https://www.facebook.com/pages/Author-Jennifer-Labelle/168414043184292

Twitter:
https://twitter.com/1JenniferLabell

Goodreads:
https://www.goodreads.com/author/show/4649930.Jennifer_Labelle

Website:
http://www.jenniferlabelle.com/

Google Plus:
https://plus.google.com/u/0/110192794885898998367/posts

BookBub:
https://www.bookbub.com/profile/jennifer-labelle

Join our Reader Group on Facebook and don't miss out on meeting our authors and entering epic giveaways!

Limitless Reading

Where reading a book is your first step to becoming *limitless...*

LIMITLESS PUBLISHING *Reader Group*

Join today! *"Where reading a book is your first step to becoming limitless..."*

https://www.facebook.com/groups/Limitless Reading/